Brutus' Journey Through The Buckeye State

Aimee Aryal

Illustrated by Justin Hilton

MASCOT BOOKS

www.mascotbooks.com

Ohio Stadium, nicknamed "The Horseshoe," hosted its first football game in 1922.

Brutus was enjoying a relaxing summer at The Ohio State University. With football season fast approaching, Brutus decided to take a journey through the Buckeye State. He was looking forward to visiting OSU fans and seeing many exciting Ohio landmarks.

From his home inside Ohio Stadium, Brutus walked across OSU's campus to University Hall where he ran into a few of his friends. The friends said, "Goodbye, Brutus! Have a nice trip!" Brutus hopped in the Buckeye Mobile and hit the road!

Brutus' first stop was the Ohio Statehouse in Columbus. Near the statue of William McKinley, some OSU fans noticed Brutus and called, "Hello, Brutus!"

Eight Ohioans have been elected President of the United States of America. They are: William H. Harrison, Ulysses S. Grant, Rutherford B. Hayes, James A. Garfield, Benjamin Harrison, William McKinley, William H. Taft, and Warren G. Harding.

Christopher Columbus set sail aboard the Santa Maria in 1492.

Brutus then visited the replica of the Santa Maria, Christopher Columbus' flagship. Brutus took the helm and imagined what it would be like to sail across the seas over 500 years ago. Brutus' mates yelled, "Ahoy, Brutus!"

Over 10,000 animals live at the Columbus Zoo and Aquarium.

Next, it was on to the world-famous Columbus Zoo and Aquarium where Brutus saw many fascinating animals. "Wow, look at those tigers, Brutus!" said a little Buckeye fan.

After a fun-filled day in Columbus, Brutus drove the Buckeye Mobile southwest on I-71. His next stop was Cincinnati, Ohio.

Fountain Square was completed in 1871.

At Fountain Square, in the heart of Cincinnati, Brutus organized an Ohio State pep rally. He led the Scarlet and Gray crowd as they sang "Across the Field" and "Buckeye Battle Cry."

From Cincinnati, Brutus headed north on I-75 to Dayton, home of Wright-Patterson Air Force Base. Brutus received a hero's welcome at the Base. Seeing the troops, Brutus felt proud to be an American.

Ohioans have played an important role in air and space travel. Dayton, Ohio residents, Wilbur and Orville Wright, built the world's first successful airplane. Neil Armstrong, born in Wapakoneta, Ohio, was the first man to walk on the moon in 1969.

A pilot invited Brutus to join him for a ride aboard a fighter jet! Brutus was a little nervous at first, but once the plane took off, he had a great time. The pilot said, "Aim high, Brutus!"

It was the hottest day of the year as Brutus continued his journey through the Buckeye State. He thought this would be a perfect day to cool off at the famous Ohio Caverns near West Liberty, Ohio. Brutus learned a lot about how the caverns and rocks were formed. As Brutus left the caverns, a family cheered, "Go Bucks!"

Regardless of weather conditions outside, the temperature inside Ohio Caverns is always 54° F.

Ready for some thrills, Brutus stopped at an amusement park in Sandusky, Ohio. He rode roller coasters all day long with Ohio State fans. Brutus felt butterflies in his stomach as he rode the coasters. OSU fans spotted Brutus and cheered, "Go, Brutus, go!"

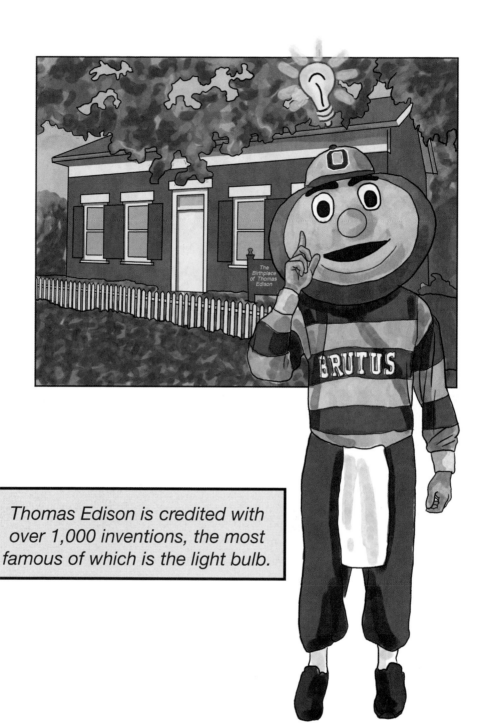

Thomas Edison is credited with over 1,000 inventions, the most famous of which is the light bulb.

Brutus' next stop was The Birthplace of Thomas Edison Museum in Milan, Ohio. Brutus learned about the amazing life of Thomas Edison, one of the most important American inventors of all time.

Next, it was on to Lake Erie. First, Brutus rented a sailboat and explored the enormous lake. Seagulls flying overhead squawked, "Hello, Brutus!"

Brutus changed out of his sailor suit and into his fishing gear. He grabbed a rod and reel and tried his hand at bass fishing. Brutus caught the biggest fish he had ever seen! In a worried voice, the fish said, "Hello, Brutus!"

Brutus was having a blast at Lake Erie! Marblehead Lighthouse was his next stop. Not surprisingly, Brutus ran into more Ohio State fans outside the lighthouse. Brutus gladly posed for pictures with his fans. The fans cheered, "Go Bucks!"

Brutus climbed to the top of the lighthouse. He was inspired by the breathtaking views of Lake Erie. Spotting Brutus atop the lighthouse, a sailor called, "Hello, Brutus!"

Built in 1822, Marblehead Lighthouse is the oldest lighthouse on the Great Lakes.

One of the American League's charter teams, the Cleveland Indians began playing in 1901.

Founded in 1918, the Cleveland Orchestra is considered one of the best orchestras in America.

Brutus' next stop was Cleveland, Ohio. There was so much to do in Cleveland! Brutus began the day by going to a Cleveland Indians baseball game. Then, Brutus led the world-famous Cleveland Orchestra as they performed for a sell-out crowd. After the performance, the crowd cheered, "Bravo, Brutus!"

The Rock and Roll Hall of Fame and Museum opened in 1995.

After conducting beautiful classical music, Brutus was ready to pick up the beat at the Rock and Roll Hall of Fame. Brutus grabbed an electric guitar and began to play. Ohio State fans cheered, "Rock on, Brutus!"

From Cleveland, Brutus headed south on I-77. He stopped at the Ohio and Erie Canal and walked along the path for several miles. Brutus passed many Buckeye fans. As people noticed Brutus, they cheered, "Hello, Brutus!"

Brutus' next stop was Canton, Ohio, home of the Pro Football Hall of Fame. Seeing so many crazy football fans reminded Brutus that Ohio State's season was starting soon. A Cleveland Browns fan barked, "Hello, Brutus!"

Sid Gillman, Lou Groza, Dante Levelli, Jim Parker, Paul Warfield, and Bill Willis are the six former Ohio State football players inducted into the Pro Football Hall of Fame.

Located in Southeastern Ohio, Wayne National Forest is the Buckeye State's only National Park.

Brutus' last stop on his journey through the Buckeye State was Wayne National Forest. Brutus hiked through the woods and came across interesting wildlife. At night, Brutus built a fire and roasted s'mores with friends.

After a tiring day, Brutus crawled into
his sleeping bag, ready for bed. As he
drifted off to sleep, he thought about the
many places he had visited on his journey
through the Buckeye State and the great
people he met along the way.

Good night, Brutus.

For Anna and Maya. ~ Aimee Aryal

For Brandon, Brooklyn, Mason, Aidan, and Brayden ~ Justin Hilton

For more information about our products,
please visit us online at www.mascotbooks.com.

Mascot Books, Inc. - P.O. Box 220157, Chantilly, VA 20153-0157

ISBN: 1-932888-70-5

Printed in the United States.

www.mascotbooks.com

Title List

Team	Book Title	Author	Team	Book Title	Author
Baseball			**Pro Football**		
Boston Red Sox	Hello, Wally!	Jerry Remy	Carolina Panthers	Let's Go, Panthers!	Aimee Aryal
Boston Red Sox	Wally And His Journey Through Red Sox Nation!	Jerry Remy	Dallas Cowboys	How 'Bout Them Cowboys!	Aimee Aryal
New York Yankees	Let's Go, Yankees!	Yogi Berra	Green Bay Packers	Go, Pack, Go!	Aimee Aryal
New York Mets	Hello, Mr. Met!	Rusty Staub	Kansas City Chiefs	Let's Go, Chiefs!	Aimee Aryal
St. Louis Cardinals	Hello, Fredbird!	Ozzie Smith	Minnesota Vikings	Let's Go, Vikings!	Aimee Aryal
Philadelphia Phillies	Hello, Phillie Phanatic!	Aimee Aryal	New York Giants	Let's Go, Giants!	Aimee Aryal
Chicago Cubs	Let's Go, Cubs!	Aimee Aryal	New England Patriots	Let's Go, Patriots!	Aimee Aryal
Chicago White Sox	Let's Go, White Sox!	Aimee Aryal	Seattle Seahawks	Let's Go, Seahawks!	Aimee Aryal
Cleveland Indians	Hello, Slider!	Bob Feller	Washington Redskins	Hail To The Redskins!	Aimee Aryal
			Coloring Book		
			Dallas Cowboys	How 'Bout Them Cowboys!	Aimee Aryal
College					
Alabama	Hello, Big Al!	Aimee Aryal	Maryland	Hello, Testudo!	Aimee Aryal
Alabama	Roll Tide!	Ken Stabler	Michigan	Let's Go, Blue!	Aimee Aryal
Arizona	Hello, Wilbur!	Lute Olson	Michigan State	Hello, Sparty!	Aimee Aryal
Arkansas	Hello, Big Red!	Aimee Aryal	Minnesota	Hello, Goldy!	Aimee Aryal
Auburn	Hello, Aubie!	Aimee Aryal	Mississippi	Hello, Colonel Rebel!	Aimee Aryal
Auburn	War Eagle!	Pat Dye	Mississippi State	Hello, Bully!	Aimee Aryal
Boston College	Hello, Baldwin!	Aimee Aryal	Missouri	Hello, Truman!	Todd Donoho
Brigham Young	Hello, Cosmo!	LaVell Edwards	Nebraska	Hello, Herbie Husker!	Aimee Aryal
Clemson	Hello, Tiger!	Aimee Aryal	North Carolina	Hello, Rameses!	Aimee Aryal
Colorado	Hello, Ralphie!	Aimee Aryal	North Carolina St.	Hello, Mr. Wuf!	Aimee Aryal
Connecticut	Hello, Jonathan!	Aimee Aryal	Notre Dame	Let's Go, Irish!	Aimee Aryal
Duke	Hello, Blue Devil!	Aimee Aryal	Ohio State	Hello, Brutus!	Aimee Aryal
Florida	Hello, Albert!	Aimee Aryal	Ohio State	Brutus' Journey	Aimee Aryal
Florida State	Let's Go, 'Noles!	Aimee Aryal	Oklahoma	Let's Go, Sooners!	Aimee Aryal
Georgia	Hello, Hairy Dawg!	Aimee Aryal	Oklahoma State	Hello, Pistol Pete!	Aimee Aryal
Georgia	How 'Bout Them Dawgs!	Vince Dooley	Penn State	Hello, Nittany Lion!	Aimee Aryal
Georgia Tech	Hello, Buzz!	Aimee Aryal	Penn State	We Are Penn State!	Joe Paterno
Gonzaga	Spike, The Gonzaga Bulldog	Mike Pringle	Purdue	Hello, Purdue Pete!	Aimee Aryal
Illinois	Let's Go, Illini!	Aimee Aryal	Rutgers	Hello, Scarlet Knight!	Aimee Aryal
Indiana	Let's Go, Hoosiers!	Aimee Aryal	South Carolina	Hello, Cocky!	Aimee Aryal
Iowa	Hello, Herky!	Aimee Aryal	So. California	Hello, Tommy Trojan!	Aimee Aryal
Iowa State	Hello, Cy!	Amy DeLashmutt	Syracuse	Hello, Otto!	Aimee Aryal
James Madison	Hello, Duke Dog!	Aimee Aryal	Tennessee	Hello, Smokey!	Aimee Aryal
Kansas	Hello, Big Jay!	Aimee Aryal	Texas	Hello, Hook 'Em!	Aimee Aryal
Kansas State	Hello, Willie!	Dan Walter	Texas A & M	Howdy, Reveille!	Aimee Aryal
Kentucky	Hello, Wildcat!	Aimee Aryal	UCLA	Hello, Joe Bruin!	Aimee Aryal
Louisiana State	Hello, Mike!	Aimee Aryal	Virginia	Hello, CavMan!	Aimee Aryal
			Virginia Tech	Hello, Hokie Bird!	Aimee Aryal
			Virginia Tech	Yea, It's Hokie Game Day!	Frank Beamer
NBA			Wake Forest	Hello, Demon Deacon!	Aimee Aryal
Dallas Mavericks	Let's Go, Mavs!	Mark Cuban	West Virginia	Hello, Mountaineer!	Aimee Aryal
Kentucky Derby			Wisconsin	Hello, Bucky!	Aimee Aryal
Kentucky Derby	White Diamond Runs For The Roses	Aimee Aryal			

More great titles coming soon!